Mama, Can Armadillos Swim?

Story by Francine Poppo Rich

Illustrations by Thomas H. Boné III & Anthony Alex LeTourneau

Blue Marlin Publications

Mama, Can Armadillos Swim?

Published by Blue Marlin Publications
Text copyright © 2004 by Francine Poppo Rich
Illustrations copyright © 2004 by Thomas H. Boné III and Anthony Alex LeTourneau
First printing 2004

Library of Congress Cataloging-in-Publication Data

Rich, Francine Poppo.
  Mama, can armadillos swim? / story by Francine Poppo Rich ; illustrations by Thomas H.
Boné III & Anthony Alex LeTourneau.
      p. cm.
  Summary: When Anna Clare seems to see various animals in or around her bathtub, she
and her mother talk about the swimming habits of mammals. Includes notes on the specific
animals mentioned.
  ISBN 0-9674602-6-3 (alk. paper)
[1. Mammals--Fiction. 2. Baths--Fiction. 3. Mothers and daughters--Fiction.] I. Boné, Thomas
H., ill. II. LeTourneau, Anthony Alex, ill. III. Title.

PZ7.R3732Mam 2004
[E]--dc22

2004010345

Blue Marlin Publications, Ltd.
823 Aberdeen Road, West Bay Shore, NY 11706
www.bluemarlinpubs.com

Book design & layout by Jude Rich

The author would like to thank the employees at the Brightwaters Post Office, especially Carla, Hilda, and Gerri.

For Anna, Our Little Angel
- FPR

To my lovely wife, Shantel, and our darling daughter Ciana, whose wonderful support helped to make my participation in this book possible.
- THB

To my boys...you have always been my teachers!
- AAL

"Oh yes. Armadillos are excellent swimmers. They look like they're going to sink. But at the last second, they gulp for air, blow up their bellies like balloons, and paddle or float across the lake or river. Sometimes, they sink to the bottom on purpose and walk under the water. They can hold their breaths under that water for up to ten minutes!"

"But not in the bathtub. Armadillos never blow up like balloons in our tub!"

"Mama, can duck-billed platypuses swim?"

"A Platypus expertly swims in rivers and streams, using its front feet to paddle and its tail to steer. Its bill has sensors for finding its favorite foods: waterworms, shrimp, and crayfish. Even in water where it can hardly see! And it loves to dive. When a platypus dives, it shuts its eyes, ears, and nostrils."

"But not in the bathtub. A Platypus may never dive into OUR tub with its eyes closed!"

"Mama, can hedgehogs swim?"

"Hedgehogs are good swimmers, but sometimes they go swimming in garden ponds and get stuck trying to swim up the slippery sides."

"But not in the bathtub. Hedgehogs never get stuck swimming up the slippery sides of our tub!"

"Mama, can rhinoceroses swim?"

"Absolutely! Rhinos love to wallow in muddy pools and sandy riverbeds. Maybe they do this because their skin is very sensitive, especially to sunburn and insect bites. Rhinos sometimes even sleep standing up in the water."

"But not in the bathtub! Rhinos never sleep standing up in our tub!"

"Hmmm...that's a tough one. Wombats live where it's pretty dry. But I've heard of a certain group of southern, hairy-nosed wombats that once built themselves a beautiful home on a hill above a big river in Australia."

"But not above the bathtub! Wombats would never build a castle above our tub!"

"Polar bears are such strong swimmers, they can swim up to 60 miles without stopping! Imagine swimming to the library sixty times without resting!"

"But not in the bathtub! Polar bears never swim sixty miles in our tub!"

"Mama, can giraffes swim?"

"Giraffes are so big, they don't need to swim. A lake is like a bathtub for a giraffe. When it does go to a lake or river, it has to take a friend. If it doesn't, a crocodile might attack it when it crouches all the way down for a drink."

"But not near the bathtub. Giraffes and their friends never crouch low next to our tub."

"Mama, can llamas swim?"

"Well, as a rule, they don't swim. They would rather jump over water than swim through it. They can learn to swim, though, especially if they are taught."

"But not in the bathtub. Nobody is teaching llamas to swim in our tub!"

"Porcupines spend most of their time climbing trees, but they love to chew on hard, oily, salty wood. They are strong swimmers, so if they spot a good piece of tree or a runaway, salty canoe paddle floating in a bay, they might swim after them."

"But not in the bathtub. Porcupines may not go fishing for salty, canoe paddles or tree branches in our tub!"

"Mama, can walruses swim?"

"Actually, walruses spend more time swimming than they do resting on ice and land. In fact, a walrus can take in a giant mouthful of water and squirt it like a hose at the sea floor to dig up clams and worms and crabs and squid."

"But not in the bathtub. No walrus is digging up clams and worms and crabs and squid from our tub!"

"Elephants like water so much that they will actually use their trunks to dig up new water holes from deep in the ground. And they love to pour water on themselves and their babies."

"But please. Please. Not in the bathtub. Elephants must never pour water on their babies in our tub!"

"Many dogs love to splash and play in pools and oceans."

"But not in the bathtub. Dogs never splash
and play in our tub! Well...maybe sometimes."

Armadillo

Armadillos have been observed taking mud baths; some scientists believe armadillos may be mini-dinosaurs, relatives of the glyptodont, a giant prehistoric animal with a natural bony shell. The water is not the only place where armadillos hold their breaths. They can hold their breaths for up to six minutes while they dig burrows deep in the dirt. They bury their noses and mouths into the dirt and dig quickly, without stopping to breathe.

Platypuses have large flaps of leathery skin on their front feet that form a paddle, propelling them through the water. These are the only mammals that have beaks like ducks, tails like beavers, and the ability to lay eggs. When the first ones were discovered 200 years ago in Australia, some scientists thought they were fakes, suspecting that someone might have sewn on the beak as a trick. But platypuses are very real!

Platypus

Hedgehogs were originally called urchins, which may explain why modern-day sea urchins resemble hedgehogs! Hedgehogs have large muscles running along their stomachs, which allow them to curl into spiky, little balls for defense. They are NOT related to porcupines. They are, however, related to the garlic-scented moonrat of Southeast Asia!

Hedgehog

Rhino

The black rhinoceros and the white rhinoceros are the same color: brownish gray! A rhino's horn is made of the same material as your hair and nails! A group of rhinos is sometimes called a crash. Can you figure out why?

Southern, Hairy-nosed Wombat

"These animals live in hot, dry South Australia. To escape the heat, they live underground and venture out, only to forage, at night. I like to think of their subterranean abodes (called warrens) as wombat castles, since they consist of interconnected passageways. Sometimes I can see multiple levels and delicate archways. The soil-heaps from their burrows are enormous and have been seen from outer space!"

Dr. Faith Walker
Department of Biological Sciences
Monash University
Victoria, Australia

Polar Bear

A polar bear actually has black skin, covered by guard hairs (clear, hollow tubes filled with air) that keep the water away from the bear's skin and trap the sunlight against his skin, just like a solar heater! These hairs seem to glisten in the same way that snow does. A mother polar bear can give birth and nurse her young while still in her winter sleep.

Giraffe

A giraffe's foot is the size of a frisbee. And its tongue is as long as two adult feet! A giraffe can skillfully use its long tongue to reach around thorns. And if it does get a thorn, its thick saliva will coat the thorn like a web! "At the Long Island Game Farm, our giraffe, Gentle Jerry, weighs over 2000 pounds and eats alfalfa hay, mixed grain water, and up to 100 pounds of carrots every day!"

Melinda Novak
Owner
Long Island Game Farm
Manorville, NY

Llama

"Most of our llamas don't like water. When we are hiking, they want to jump over the creek, no matter how wide it is. It takes quite a while to teach them that it is actually safe to walk through a creek. We even have to teach them how to drink from the running water of a creek because all their lives, they have drunk from a water trough or bucket!"

> Brian Pinkerton
> Mount Lehman Llamas
> B.C., Canada

Porcupine

The porcupine is the second largest of all rodents. The beaver is the largest. Those pointy things (porcupines have about 30,000 pointy things!) on their backs and tails are called quills.

"I work in the mountains of southern Tanzania where I study animals and plants that live there, and I help the local people protect their forests. Porcupines live in many parts of Tanzania, and they are known in the language of Swahili as Nungunungu. They are shy animals and are rarely seen. One day I was walking with some villagers in a remote forest when, suddenly, we heard a strange noise. It sounded like someone was shaking a box of beans. We walked around a large sugarbush, and there on the trail was a porcupine, staring at us and waggling his backside very enthusiastically. He looked like he was drying himself off after a swim. But in fact he was shaking the hollow rattle-quills on his tail, and this strange noise was intended to scare us away. On seeing people all around him, the porcupine just waggled more fiercely. He then began to dance round and round in circles, faster and faster. The noise of the rattles, the dance, and the sharp quills pointing straight at us made us laugh, and we left the porcupine to wander off safely into the forest."

> Tim Davenport
> Director, Southern Highlands Conservation Program
> Wildlife Conservation Society
> Tanzania

Walrus

Walruses use their whiskers to locate their food. Their bodies are also designed for lots of good diving. After diving, they can remain under water for ten minutes before they have to come up for a breath. Walruses are marine mammals, and all marine mammals have to breathe outside the water.

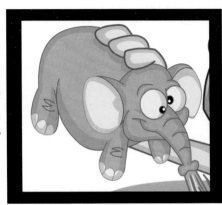

Elephants are sometimes called pachyderms. This means "thick skin." An elephant's trunk is its upper lip AND its nose. An elephant's trunk is so strong, it could push a car! An it uses that same trunk to pull in up to three gallons of water at once. That's probably more water than your whole family drinks in a week!

Elephant

Dog

Dogs...you already know all about dogs!

Can You Believe How Much You Know About Mammals?

All the animals discussed in this book are mammals. There are three different types, or classes, of mammals. **Monotremes** have hair and produce milk for their young, but they also lay eggs. Duck-billed platypuses are **monotremes**. **Marsupials** grow inside the mother's body, not in an egg. When they are born, they are tiny and undeveloped. They climb into the mother's pouch and settle inside, where they can drink the mother's milk until they are grown enough to come out. Southern, hairy-nosed wombats are **marsupials**. **Placental** mammals develop inside the mother's body and are able to exist separate from the mother's body when they are born. You are a **placental** mammal. And so are many of the mammals in this book!

You know so much about mammals now, you can probably answer all these questions. If not, you'll find the answers somewhere within this book.

1. I am a marathon swimmer. I can swim sixty miles without resting. That means that if I lived in New York, I could swim to New Jersey. What am I?

2. I have a special muscle that runs along my stomach, which allows me to curl up into a spiky ball when I am afraid. What am I?

3. Have you ever tried to dig a burrow so deep in the ground that your nose and mouth are completely covered with dirt? It's not easy, but I can do it. What am I?

4. I am a special kind of mammal called a monotreme. What am I?

5. I bring friends with me to the watering hole because I have to watch out for hungry crocodiles. What am I?

6. I live in a country called Australia. And I am a special kind of mammal called a marsupial. I could be a kangaroo, but I am not. What am I?

7. I can sleep standing up in the water. What am I?

8. I love to gnaw on salty things. What am I?

9. I don't like to swim. I'd rather try to jump over a creek. What am I?

10. I clean my baby by pouring water all over her with my trunk. What am I?

11. My favorite foods are worms, crabs and squid. What am I?